BAKUGAN
BATTLE BRAWLERS

MASQUERADE
BRAWL

Adapted by Tracey West

D0958090

SCHOLASTIC INC.
New York   Toronto   London   Auckland
Sydney   Mexico City   New Delhi   Hong Kong

ISBN-13: 978-0-545-13121-6   ISBN-10: 0-545-13121-9
© Spin Master Ltd/Sega Toys.
BAKUGAN and BATTLE BRAWLERS, and all related titles, logos, and characters are trademarks of Spin Master LTD.
NELVANA is a trademark of Nelvana Limited. CORUS is a trademark of Corus Entertainment Inc.
Used under license by Scholastic Inc. All Rights Reserved.
Published by Scholastic Inc. SCHOLASTIC and associated logos are trademarks
and/or registered trademarks of Scholastic Inc.
12 11 10 9 8 7 6 5 4 3 2 1   9 10 11 12 13 14/0
Illustrated by Carlo LoRaso and Steve Haefele
Printed in the U.S.A.
First printing, September 2009

Drago is a Pyrus Dragonoid, a red Bakugan with huge wings.
He comes from Vestroia, the home of all Bakugan.

Drago became Dan's Bakugan. Drago had even spoken to Dan once, during a battle! But Drago didn't want to be owned by a human. He wanted to get back to Vestroia.

Dan didn't know any of that. So he brought Drago to school with him to show him off.

"Feast your eyes on the one and only Drago, guys," Dan bragged.

"Is that the one that talks?" asked a short boy with spiky hair.
"Hey, Dan, make it say something!" said another boy.
"I'm so jealous," a girl said. "Mine has not said one word yet."

One boy didn't believe Dan. "Maybe you just made the whole thing up, Danny!" he said. Dan smiled. "I'll prove it to you, all right?

"Ready, Drago?" Dan asked. "It's showtime!" Dan tossed the red Bakugan ball in the air. "Bakugan Stand!"

He tried again and again, but Drago didn't move or talk. The kids were disappointed. "Maybe it's busted," a boy said.

Dan bent down and whispered into the Bakugan ball. "You're embarrassing me, Drago," he hissed.

Dan was still upset with Drago after school. "Thanks for wrecking my life, Drago! All you had to do was talk. I wonder if all the other brawlers out there have such a stubborn Bakugan."

But when Dan logged on, he found out that lots of brawlers didn't have their Bakugan anymore! Someone named Masquerade was stealing Bakugan during battles. Runo had even lost Terrorclaw.

"We have to do something, Dan," Marucho said. Dan agreed. "Don't worry, guys, you can count on me. I'm going to put my own Bakugan on the line and challenge Masquerade!"

A voice piped up next to Dan. It was Drago! "Is this all just a game to you?" Drago asked.

"Hello! This is the greatest game ever!" Dan said.

"Whoa, did you just talk, Drago?"

"Listen to me, human. I am not a toy," Drago said, rolling closed again. "Bakugan is more than a game."

But Dan didn't listen to Drago's warning. He challenged Masquerade anyway. Nobody bullied the brawlers and got away with it!

The next day, Dan was ready to battle. So was Masquerade. "Field Open! Gate Card Set!" the brawlers shouted.

Masquerade threw another card onto the field, too. "Your move," he said.

Dan wasn't sure what Masquerade had thrown down, but he decided to use Serpenoid. "Bakugan Stand!" he yelled.

Masquerade used Reaper, an evil-looking Darkus
beast with ragged wings and big horns.
Dan wasn't worried. He knew Serpenoid would still
win. But then Masquerade played an Ability Card Dan
had never seen before. It was called Dimension Four.

Suddenly, Dan's G-Power points dropped, and Reaper used his weapon to cut a hole in the battle space above Serpenoid. Dan's Bakugan was sucked through the hole.

"Oh no!" Dan cried. "He took my beast right out of the battle!"

Dan wasn't giving up. He threw down Saurus. But Masquerade was prepared, and played another special card, Double Dimension. Saurus vanished just like Serpenoid!

"No fair! I want my Bakugan back!" Dan cried.
"Sorry," Masquerade said. "Once the Doom Card is played, the battle is over."

"The Doom Card overpowers all cards and sends the defeated Bakugan into another dimension forever," Masquerade explained. Drago spoke up. "He's right, human. A Bakugan can never return from the Doom Dimension."

"Now I know how you're stealing everyone's Bakugan," Dan said. "But why are you wrecking our game?" Masquerade smiled. "Who said this was just a game? Every single battle is real."

Every single battle is real, Dan thought. Drago had told him the same thing!
Dan had one more chance. He couldn't lose now!

Reaper and Drago faced each other on the field. But this time, Masquerade's plan didn't work. Dan's last card broke apart in his hand as the Bakugan field exploded.

Once the field had disappeared, Dan was relieved to find Drago's Bakugan ball. He hadn't won the brawl, but at least he still had Drago!

"Bakugan is not a game. It's a battle that can lead to the destruction of the entire world," Masquerade said, smiling. "And the only way to stop it is for you to defeat me."

Dan knew this wasn't the last time he'd see the mysterious brawler. And if it was up to him to save the world, he would be ready.

"I will beat you, Masquerade!"